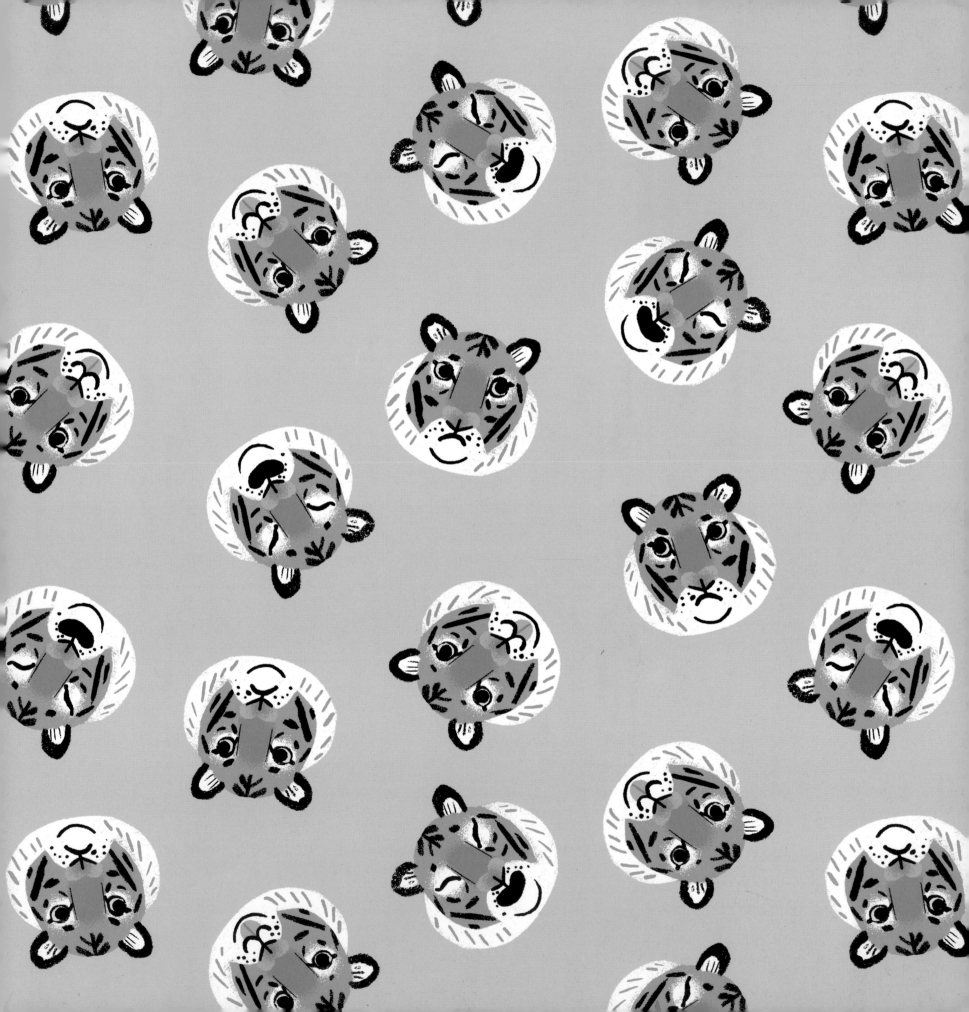

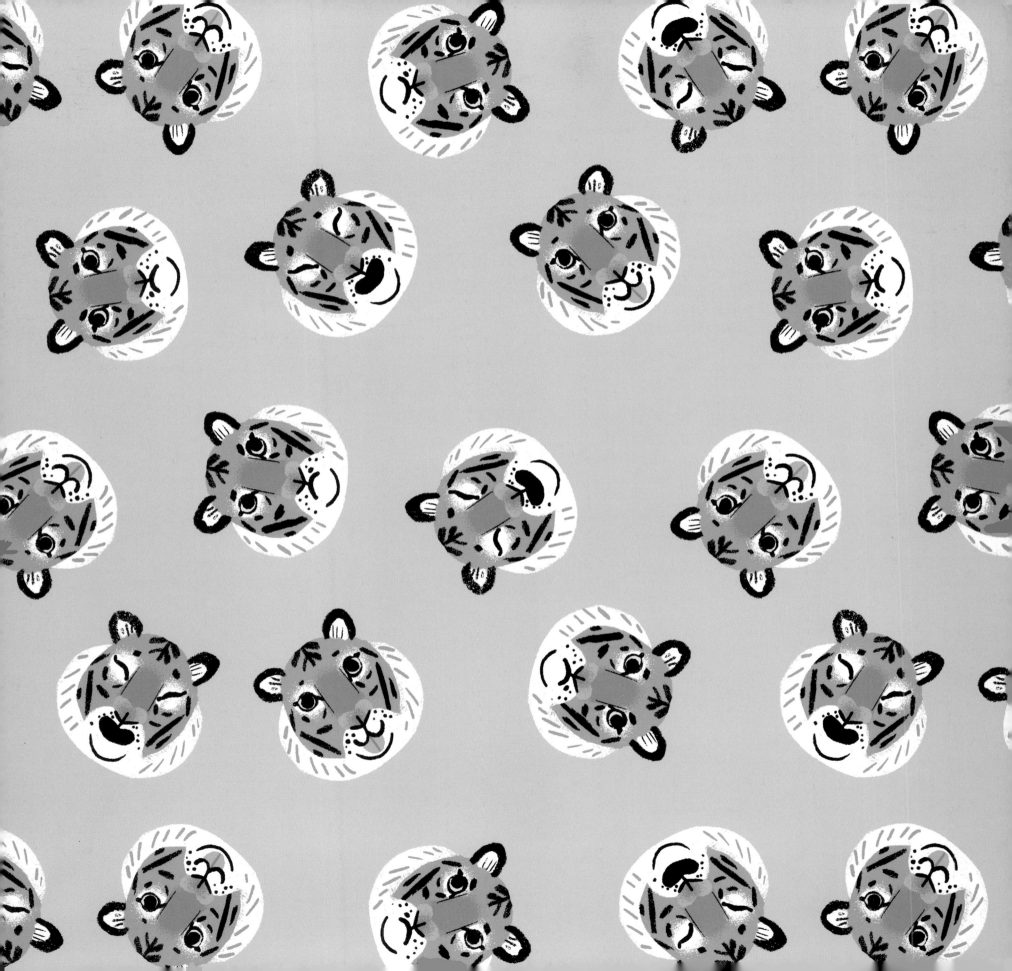

HODDER CHILDREN'S BOOKS

First published in hardback in Great Britain in 2020
by Hodder and Stoughton

This paperback edition published in 2021

A CIP catalogue record of this book
is available from the British Library.

ISBN: 978 1 444 94647 5

10 9 8 7 6 5 4 3 2 1

Printed and bound in China.

Hodder Children's Books
An imprint of
Hachette Children's Group
Part of Hodder and Stoughton
Carmelite House
50 Victoria Embankment
London, EC4Y 0DZ

An Hachette UK Company
www.hachette.co.uk

www.hachettechildrens.co.uk

Today I'M STRONG

Written by

Nadiya Hussain

Illustrated by

Ella Bailey

Hodder Children's Books

I love to go to school. Well, most days I do.
There are some days when what I *really* want
is to stay at home with you.

Because I can tell you everything and I know you listen.
Even when you don't say a word.

I love to go to school. I do.
Mrs Reid smiles when I get
there early, and I run with
Lucas and Muna through
the clanging gates.

I love to go to school. I do.

In class we write about our favourite things,
and I tell my friends all about you.

I love to go to school. I really do.

I wait for the bell at the end of every class
so I can race for the door and run out into the playground,

faster than fast,
and up nearly to the top
of the climbing frame.

But some days ...

. . . I don't like it so much.

Some days, I just don't want to go. And that's when I don't say a word.
My voice just disappears. Because some days, school feels sad.

Sometimes I can feel Molly staring at me.

Sometimes Molly laughs at my stories, but not in a good way.

Sometimes she stands in front of me, blocking my way, and I don't feel like going on the climbing frame.

And sometimes, Molly says,
"That cake is mine. You've got enough!"

That's when I can't find my voice.
That's when I want to hide.

I like going to school, most days I do.
But not always.

But today, something wonderful happened …
When Molly was mean, I thought of YOU.

And then I knew exactly what to do.

Molly shouldn't block my way,
or stop me from playing,
or take my food.

It's not OK to be mean.

To make faces.

To hold on too tight.

To say words that hurt.

I love to go to school. And today I found my voice.
You showed that it was hiding inside of me all the time.

I walked past Molly. When she laughed, I didn't even look.

At break time, I walked past Molly's blocking arms.
"Today, I'm going to the top of the climbing frame,"
I told her.

And soon I'm going to be on top of the world.

Maybe not today.

But some day very soon.

Like tomorrow.

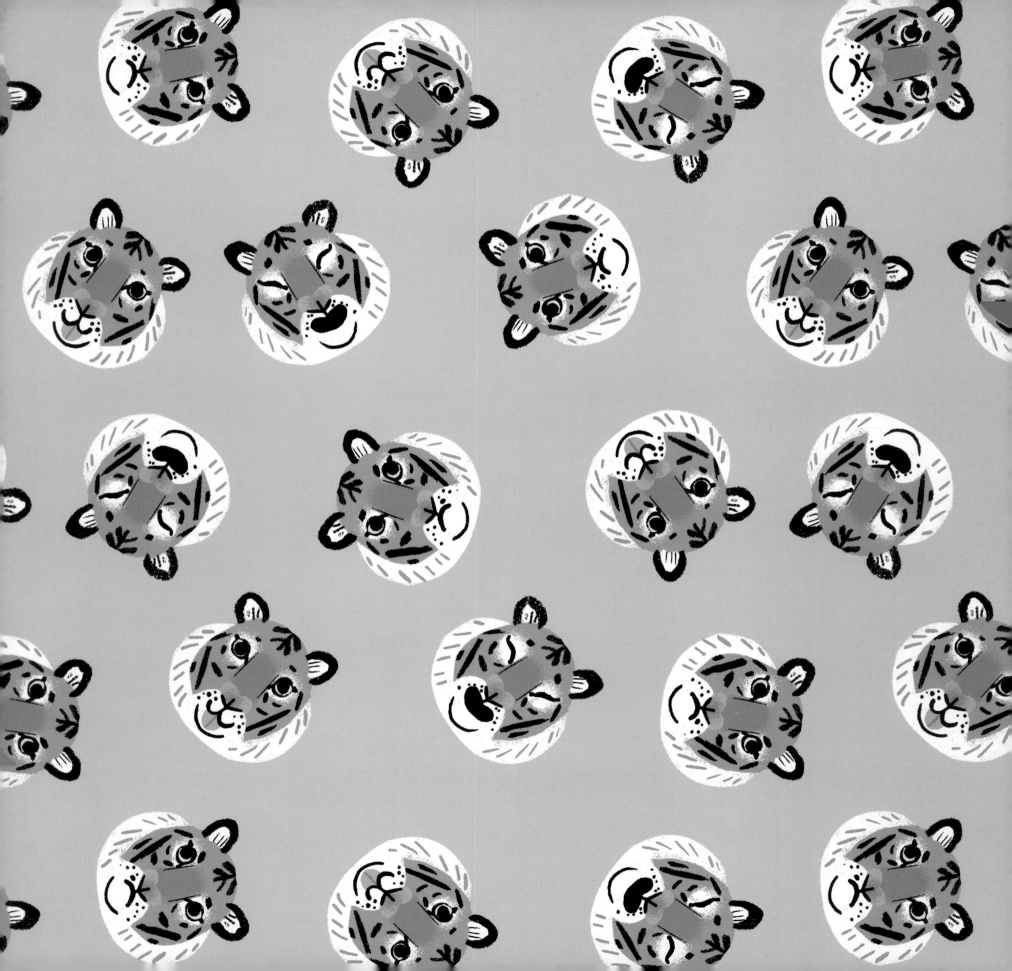

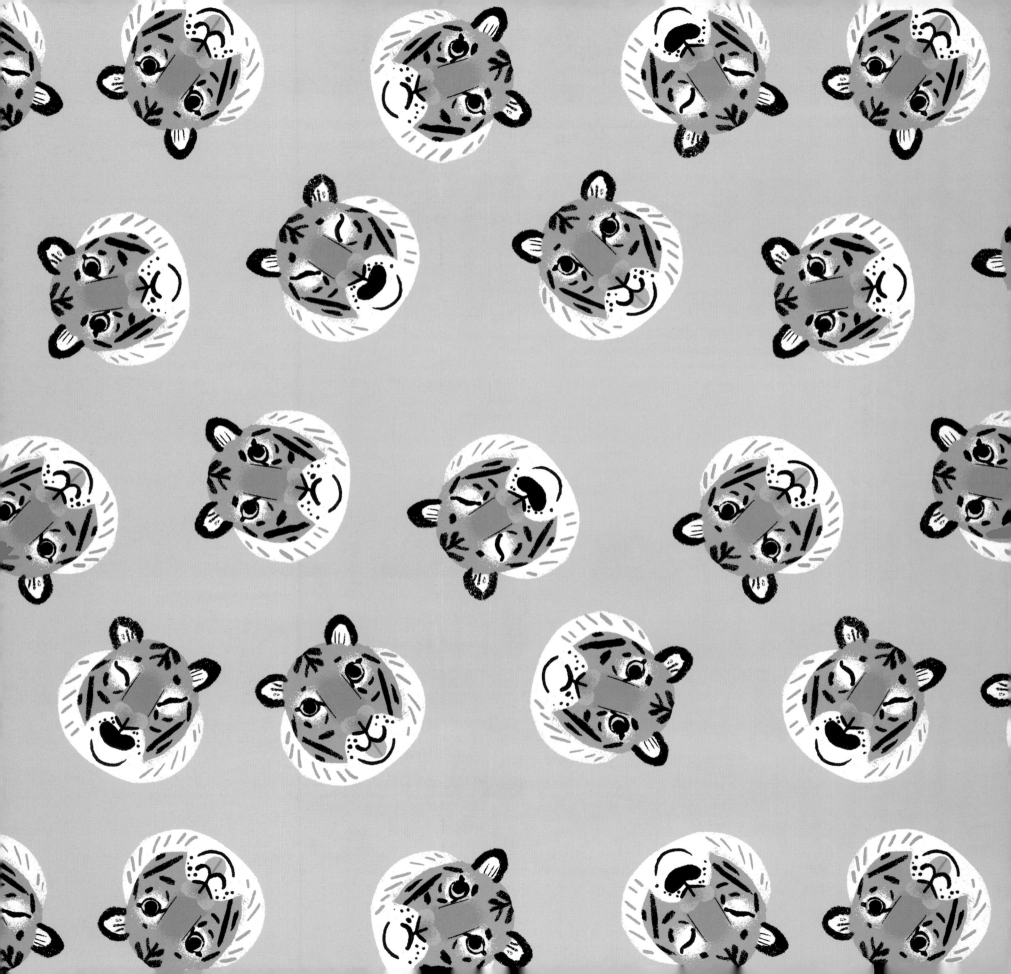